Freddie Fernortner

FEARLESS FIRST GRADER ®

An AudioCraft Publishing, Inc. book

Freddie Fernortner, Fearless First Grader©
#1: The Fantastic Flying Bicycle
Paperback edition ISBN 978-1-893699-78-6

Illustrations by Cartoon Studios, Battle Creek, Michigan

Visit www.freddiefernortner.com

Printed in the USA

THE FANTASTIC FLYING BICYCLE

1

The story of Freddie Fernortner is a curious one. Oh, sure, he was in many ways a very normal first grader . . . with a few exceptions.

For one, Freddie was very, very smart. When he was just one year old, he could speak very clearly. At two, he knew his ABCs. And when he was only three, he knew the names of every single state in America.

His mother and father were quite

proud. His mother would often look at him and say, "My goodness, Freddie! You're the smartest boy in the city!"

This made Freddie feel very good.

But Freddie Fernortner also had a very, very active imagination—a fearless imagination—which, unfortunately, often got him into trouble.

And not just him, either. You see, Freddie had three best friends: Darla, his next door neighbor; Chipper, his friend from across the street; and Mr. Chewy, Freddie's cat. The cat was named Mr. Chewy because Freddie had taught the creature to chew bubble gum. Mr. Chewy could even blow bubbles!

Freddie, Darla, Chipper, and Mr. Chewy were the best of friends . . . which meant that when Freddie got into trouble, so did Darla and Chipper and Mr. Chewy.

And once again, Freddie, Darla, Chipper, and Mr. Chewy were about to find themselves in an awful lot of trouble. In fact, what was about to happen to Freddie and his friends would be one of the scariest things that had ever happened to them.

2

It was Saturday morning. Freddie was sitting on his front porch, watching a small bird chase a butterfly. Mr. Chewy sat at Freddie's feet, chewing gum and blowing bubbles. The sun peeked up over the trees, and the morning air was cool.

Suddenly, Darla called out from her bedroom window.

"Hey Freddie!" she said. "Do you want to go for a bike ride?"

Freddie leapt to his feet. "Sure!" he said. "Let's see if Chipper wants to go, too!"

Seconds later, Darla emerged from her house and met up with Freddie and Mr. Chewy on the sidewalk that snaked along Fudgewhipple Street. The pair walked across the street and knocked on Chipper's door. After a few minutes, the door opened. Chipper was there.

"Do you want to go for a bike ride?" Freddie asked.

"That would be fun!" Chipper said. "We can race each other to the park. Why, I can pedal so fast that I can almost fly!"

Which got Freddie thinking.

"You know," he said as he turned and stared up into the bright blue sky, "I bet we really *could* fly. I mean . . . if we worked really hard."

"What do you mean?" Darla asked.

Freddie was getting more and more excited by the second.

"We can put wings on my bike," he explained. "And we can hook up a fan to the chain! The fan will power the bike, and we can steer with the wings!" Freddie stretched out his arms like a plane and ran around in circles. "It'll be a fantastic flying bicycle!" he exclaimed.

Chipper scratched his head. "Do you really think it'll work?" he asked, raising one eyebrow.

"Yeah," Darla said. "It sounds scary."

Freddie stopped running around in circles. His arms fell to his sides. "It won't be scary!" he said. "We can make wings out of wood! And my dad has an old fan in the garage! We can make it work!"

And that was that. Freddie, Chipper,

and Darla went to Freddie's garage and got to work on the fantastic flying bicycle. All the while, Mr. Chewy sat nearby, watching, chewing gum, and blowing an occasional bubble.

Two hours later they were finished, and the three friends stood around the fantastic flying machine. A big house fan was mounted behind the seat. Wings made of wood were connected to the handlebars with ropes, so the craft could be steered by turning left or right. Freddie attached a small leather tool bag beneath the fan, in case they needed to make any adjustments or repairs.

"It looks cool," Darla said.

"Super cool," Chipper agreed.

"It looks super-duper cool," Freddie said. "Who wants to be the first to try it out?"

"Not me," Darla said, taking a step back. "I've never flown before."

"Me neither," Chipper said, shaking his head. "It was your idea, Freddie. *You* try it out."

Freddie shrugged. Then he looked up at the blue sky. Several large, puffy, white clouds loomed in the distance. There was a sharp, snapping sound as Mr. Chewy popped a bubble.

"Looks like a good day to fly a bike," Freddie said.

He hopped on the fantastic flying bicycle.

He started pedaling.

The fan blades started whirring.

Faster.

Faster still.

The bike began moving forward.

Faster . . . .

Question was: would it really fly?

Freddie Fernortner, fearless first grader, was about to find out.

3

The fan blades on the back of the bike whirred, pushing the bike faster and faster down the street.

"Come on, Freddie!" Chipper shouted, thrusting his fists into the air. "Let's see you fly!"

"Yeah!" Darla cheered. "You can do it, Freddie!"

And suddenly, it happened.

The front tire of the bicycle left the

ground.

Freddie pedaled faster.

"He's going to do it!" Chipper exclaimed in disbelief. "He's really going to do it!"

The rear wheel of the bike left the ground.

Freddie was flying!

The bike rose into the air. In no time at all, Freddie and the fantastic flying bicycle were above the trees, soaring like an eagle above Fudgewhipple Street and over the neighborhood.

Darla cheered. Chipper cheered. Mr. Chewy sat next to a tree, chomping on a wad of gum, watching the strange flying machine circling above.

"See!?!?" Freddie exclaimed, his voice booming down. "I knew it would work! I just *knew* it!"

Freddie began pedaling slower, and the fantastic flying bicycle began to lower. Freddie landed on the sidewalk and the bike coasted up to his friends.

"That was cool!" he exclaimed. "Do you want to try it, Chipper?"

Chipper looked wary. "I don't

know," he said, glancing up into the air. "I'm afraid of heights."

"Darla?" Freddie asked.

Darla, too, was a little nervous. "I will," she said, "but only if you go with me, Freddie. Do you think we both could ride it?"

"I think so," Freddie said, scooting forward on the seat. "Hop on."

Darla swung her leg up and sat on the seat behind Freddie. She wrapped her arms around his waist.

"Hang on tight!" Freddie ordered. "We're going to fly!"

And he started pedaling . . . not knowing that disaster was about to strike.

4

Freddie pedaled very fast.

The bike raced down the street.

But it didn't fly.

"Maybe I'm too heavy!" Darla shouted as the wind rushed past. "I had a big bowl of cereal for breakfast, you know!"

"We can do it!" shouted Freddie.

He pedaled faster.

Faster.

The front tire rose.

Then the rear tire.

"Woo-hoo, Freddie!" Darla shouted with glee. The wind whipped at her hair. "We're flying! We're really flying!"

The bike rose higher. Freddie turned the handlebars to the right, and the fantastic flying bicycle began to circle back.

"Look at Chipper!" Freddie shouted. "He looks like an ant from up here!"

"Mr. Chewy looks like a little speck," Darla said. "Hi Chipper! Hi Mr. Chewy!"

Higher and higher they circled. They could see all of the houses on Fudgewhipple Street, and even buildings in the nearby city. A seagull wheeled past, screeched once, and gave Freddie and Darla a funny look.

"Let's go back down," Freddie said. "I'll bet that Chipper will change his mind when he sees how much fun this is. He'll want to go for a ride, too!"

Freddie's legs slowed on the pedals, and the fantastic flying bicycle began to coast toward the ground.

Suddenly, a gust of wind caught the bike, causing it to lean sharply to the right. Darla squeezed Freddie.

"Hang on tight!" Freddie shouted. "It's getting windy!"

He regained control of the craft, steering it toward the sidewalk below. Ahead, on the ground, he saw Chipper and Mr. Chewy standing near the street, watching.

The fantastic flying bicycle dropped lower. They were now only a few feet from the ground.

Another gust of wind caught the craft, raising it into the air. Freddie and Darla were jolted on the seat.

"Hang on!" Freddie repeated. "The wind is getting worse!"

The bike lurched to the left, then to the right, caught in the strong gust of wind.

"Land! Land!" Darla screeched.

"I'm . . . I'm trying!" Freddie stammered. "But . . . but the wind is . . . is just too . . . too . . . strong!"

Chipper was watching as the fantastic flying bicycle came closer and closer. He could tell that Freddie was having a hard time landing.

"I'll catch you!" he shouted bravely as the flying bike came toward him. The bike suddenly buzzed over his head. Chipper leapt, reaching for the bicycle.

But—

He missed, and the craft continued bobbling in the air, several feet above the sidewalk.

Chipper gave chase, racing after the bicycle, leaping into the air, trying to grasp the bike and pull his friends down. Mr. Chewy followed at his heels, scampering along the sidewalk and chewing a wad of gum.

And what a sight it was! Freddie and Darla, seated on the fantastic flying bicycle, and Chipper, running as fast as his legs would carry him, leaping up into the air, desperately trying to pull his friends safely down to earth.

"If . . . I . . . could . . . only . . . get . . . a . . . hold . . . of . . . it!" Chipper stammered as he jumped and ran. "Then . . . I . . . could . . . pull . . . you . . . down!"

Suddenly—

Success!

Chipper's hand grasped the bottom bar of the bike.

He held on tight and pulled with all of his might.

But a terrible thing happened.

Just as he grabbed the bike, another gust of wind seized the craft.

A *strong* gust of wind.

Darla screamed.

Freddie screamed.

Chipper screamed as he was pulled up into the air! He held the bike with one hand and swung madly with his free arm. Mr. Chewy leapt into the air and Chipper caught him by the tail.

And the wind continued to blow.

Harder.

Stronger.

There was nothing any of them could do as the fantastic flying bicycle carried Freddie, Darla, Chipper, and Mr. Chewy higher and higher, into the sky.

"Oh, man!" Freddie gasped. "We're in trouble now!"

"Big trouble!" Darla shrieked.

"*Huge* trouble!" Chipper shouted from beneath them.

Of course, Freddie, Darla, and Chipper had no way of knowing it, but their troubles were only *beginning*.

5

The fantastic flying bicycle rose higher and higher. Houses and buildings below looked smaller and smaller.

"Chipper!" Freddie shouted as he glanced down. "Are you okay?!?!"

"Yeah!" Chipper replied. "But I don't think Mr. Chewy is enjoying the ride!"

"Climb up here!" Freddie ordered, "before you and Mr. Chewy fall!"

It took a lot of work, but Chipper

managed to scramble up over the wing. He handed Mr. Chewy to Darla and squeezed behind her on the seat.

"This is just awful!" Darla shouted above the rushing wind. "We've got to land!"

"I'm trying!" Freddie shouted back. "But the wind is too strong!"

Suddenly, they were in a large cloud. The ground beneath them disappeared. The blue sky around them vanished. The only thing they could see was a foggy white mist.

"This is weird," Chipper said as he looked around. "I've never been in a cloud before."

"Me neither," Darla said.

"Well, at least we're not bouncing all around anymore," Freddie said. He pedaled harder and found that he was able to steer. "The wind has died down," he continued. "Maybe we can make it back to the ground now."

"I can't even *see* the ground," Chipper said, looking down. "The only thing I can see is this cloud."

"We'll come out of it soon," Freddie said. "Then we'll be able to see where we are. As long as it doesn't get windy again, we should be able to land."

On and on they flew.

"This must be a huge cloud," Darla said. "We've been flying for days and days."

Actually, it had only been a few minutes . . . but for Freddie, Darla, and Chipper, it sure *seemed* like days. After all, flying a bicycle through a cloud is a pretty scary experience.

They flew and flew, farther and

farther. Still, the cloud surrounded them like a misty white curtain.

It wasn't long, however, before they heard something.

A noise in the cloud.

A steady roar. It was faint at first, but it was getting louder.

Closer.

Suddenly, Darla thrust out her arm and pointed over Freddie's shoulder.

"Oh my gosh!" she shrieked. "It's a plane!"

Darla was right. A large plane suddenly appeared through the clouds. It was moving super-fast . . . *and it was headed right for them!*

6

The sight was horrifying. Freddie, Darla, Chipper, and Mr. Chewy were seated on the fantastic flying bicycle . . . heading right into the path of the oncoming plane!

"We're going to crash!" Chipper howled, and he threw his hands over his face to cover his eyes. Darla placed her hands over Freddie's eyes and buried her face into his shoulder so she wouldn't see. Even Mr. Chewy covered his eyes with his paws.

The roaring of the plane grew deafening. Louder, louder . . . .

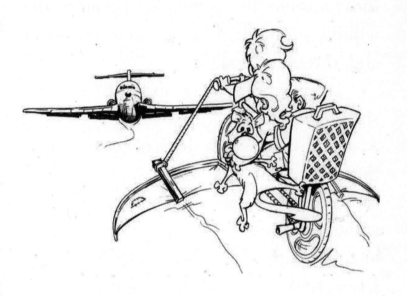

And then—

It was gone!

At the very last possible second, the pilot spotted the flying bike and its terrified passengers. He had been able to steer the plane away, missing Freddie, Darla, Chipper, and Mr. Chewy by only inches!

But the worst wasn't over just yet.

The wind created by the plane sent the fantastic flying bicycle swirling and whirling, tumbling and turning, end over end, through the sky.

"Everybody hang on tight!" Freddie shrieked.

Mr. Chewy was suddenly tossed from the bike, but Darla reached out and scooped up the cat with her arm before the animal was lost. Mr. Chewy accidentally lost his gum. The tiny pink wad went flying, hurdling back toward the earth.

Finally, Freddie regained control of the bicycle.

"That was close," he said.

"I thought we were goners!" Chipper exclaimed. "I thought we were going to crash right into that plane!"

And suddenly, a piece of blue sky appeared above them. The canopy of white began to break apart. Far below, ground appeared.

"We're coming out of the cloud!" Freddie shouted. "Now we can go home!"

He steered the fantastic flying bicycle to the right and began to circle back. The craft began to drop, faster and faster.

"Hey, hey, not so fast," Chipper said.

"I . . . I'm trying," Freddie said, pedaling faster. "But something's not right. I'm pedaling as hard as I can, but we're still falling really fast."

Chipper turned around and looked at the fan behind him. "Well, you might be pedaling," he said, "but the fan blades aren't turning."

Suddenly, Freddie looked down.

He gasped.

"Oh, no!" he cried. "The chain! The chain is broken! There's no way to power the fan!"

"If you can't power the fan," Darla said, "how are you going to keep the bike flying?"

"That's what I mean!" Freddie shrieked. "I don't have any way of powering the bike!"

It was terrible news. They'd been very lucky so far, and for a moment, Freddie, Darla, and Chipper thought that they would make it safely back to earth.

Now, however, they knew there was nothing they could do as the fantastic flying bicycle plummeted faster and faster toward the ground.

The three friends—and Mr. Chewy, too—knew that their luck had just run out.

7

Freddie, Darla, and Chipper were screaming at the top of their lungs. Even Mr. Chewy was wailing, meowing as loud as his little cat-mouth would allow.

And all the while, the fantastic flying bicycle fell faster and faster toward the ground.

"We're going to be smashed flat as a pancake!" Darla screeched. "My mom and dad are going to be really, really mad!"

"I'm probably going to be grounded!" Chipper said.

"How can you be grounded if you're flat as a pancake?!?!" Freddie shouted.

Chipper had to think about that for a moment. "Yeah, I guess you're right," he finally replied.

"Do something!" Darla demanded.

"There's nothing I can do!" Freddie answered. "The only thing we can do is hope that we land somewhere soft, like a haystack."

"But there aren't any farms around here," Darla said.

"It's too bad we couldn't soar like a bird," Chipper said.

"You know," Freddie said as he turned the handlebars, "maybe we *can* soar like a bird. Maybe if I steer us around and around in circles, we could catch some wind."

"But we'd still be going down," Chipper said.

"Sure," Freddie agreed, turning the handlebars even more. "But at least we won't be dropping *straight* down. Maybe we could soar in circles and make a soft landing."

And his idea worked.

As the fantastic flying bicycle began to circle around and around, it was no longer dropping as quickly as it had been.

"You're doing it, Freddie!" Darla cheered, hugging Mr. Chewy tightly. "We're going to live, after all!"

"Yeah," Chipper chimed in, "as long as we can stay away from airplanes."

"Uh oh," Freddie said. "We've got more trouble. Look below us."

"It's a lake," Darla said. "Can you

steer us around it?"

"I'm trying," Freddie replied as he struggled with the handlebars.

Indeed, the three were in deep trouble. The fantastic flying bicycle was circling around and around, falling toward the earth. But while Freddie had *some* control of the craft, he could only steer it around and around . . . otherwise, the bicycle would lose its lift, and it would once again begin to plummet straight toward the lake.

"We can't land in the lake, Freddie!" Darla shouted. "There might be sharks in it!"

"There aren't any sharks in the lake!" Freddie shouted back.

"Yes, there are," Darla replied. "My big brother caught one. He said it was bigger than he was!"

"You're brother was only trying to scare you," Chipper said. "Sharks only live in the ocean."

"Chipper's right," Freddie said. "There aren't any sharks in the lake."

The lake below was a field of shimmering blue, looming closer and closer.

"Everybody get ready," Freddie ordered. "We're going to land in the water, but I think I can steer us so we're close to the shore. Hang on to Mr. Chewy, Darla."

"Did I mention that I don't ever want to do this again?" Chipper shouted over the rushing wind.

The fantastic flying bicycle circled, dropping lower with every turn.

Lower . . . .

Lower still . . . .

Until—

Splash!

The bicycle and the three first graders plunged into the water.

Freddie spluttered to the surface, followed by Darla. Mr. Chewy was clinging to her shirt. His fur was soaked, and he didn't look very happy at all. Mr. Chewy didn't like to get wet.

Then Chipper surfaced, coughing and spitting out water.

"We're alive!" Freddie exclaimed. "And look!" He stood up. "The water only comes up to my waist! We can walk to shore, and push the bicycle with us!"

"I sure am glad to be back on the ground, even if we *are* in a lake," Darla said, clutching Mr. Chewy. She raised her other hand and pulled a lock of wet hair from her face.

She looked down into the water.

She froze.

Her eyes widened, filled with fear. All the color drained from her face.

Then she screamed and pointed to a long, skinny shape that was right in front of her.

"A giant water snake!" she shrieked. *"It's coming after me!"*

8

Freddie spun.

Chipper gasped.

Then the two boys laughed.

"That's not a snake!" Freddie said. "It's just a stick!"

He waded over to Darla and stuck his hand into the water. "See?" he said as he pulled out the long, soggy branch. "It's just a stick. Nothing to worry about."

Darla looked relieved.

"But we *do* have something to worry about, Freddie," Chipper said. "We have no idea where we are. We're lost."

The three looked around. The lake was surrounded by trees. There were no houses around, and no people at all.

"Well, maybe we can fix the bike," Freddie said. "Then we can fly into the air, just high enough to see where we are. We might even be able to see our houses."

"I'm not going flying again," Chipper said, shaking his head. "Huh-uh, no way, not ever."

"We'll be more careful next time," Freddie said. "We won't fly very high. Come on. Help me get the bike to shore."

It was difficult. Freddie and Chipper grunted and groaned as they pushed the bicycle through the water. Darla carried Mr. Chewy in one arm, and helped push the bike with the other.

Finally, they made it to shore.

"I'm glad I've got my tool kit," Freddie said, unsnapping the small leather bag from beneath the fan. "Without tools, we'd really be in a jam."

Darla placed Mr. Chewy on the ground. The cat shook water from his fur coat, then sat down next to Freddie and meowed.

"Sorry," Freddie said to the cat. "I'm all out of gum. You're going to have to wait until we get home."

Then Freddie got to work repairing the chain. It was harder than it looked, and after a little while, Chipper announced that he was bored.

"We could go for a walk," Darla said to Chipper. "Maybe we'll find a house or something."

"Just don't go too far," Freddie said. "I'll be finished pretty soon and we can take off again."

Chipper and Darla walked along the edge of the lake. Then they disappeared into the woods. Mr. Chewy remained seated near Freddie, watching him work on the bicycle.

"There," Freddie said finally, with a

final turn of his screwdriver. "All fixed."

He looked around. There was no sign of Darla and Chipper.

"Darla!" he called. *"Chipper! The bicycle is fixed! We can go home now!"*

Still, there was no sign of his two friends. He was just about to call out again when he saw a flash of movement in the distance. It was Chipper, and he was running. Darla appeared right behind him. Both were running frantically.

Good, Freddie thought. *They heard me.*

But in the next instant, he realized that something was really, really wrong.

Darla and Chipper weren't running because they heard Freddie's shouts. They were running because something was chasing them . . . *and that something was a bear!*

9

"Holy cow!" Freddie shrieked.

He bent over and scooped up Mr. Chewy. "Hang on, buddy," he said. Then he leapt onto the fantastic flying bicycle.

"Hurry!" he shouted.

Darla and Chipper were running as fast as they could. The bear was some distance away, but it was still coming after them. It was big and black and hairy.

And scary.

Freddy gripped the handlebars with one hand, carrying Mr. Chewy in the other. He hoped that Darla and Chipper would make it to the bicycle in time for them to take off . . . and leave the bear behind.

But if his plan failed . . . .

"*Freddie!*" Chipper shouted. "*Don't leave us! Don't leave us!*"

"*I'm not!*" Freddie shouted back. "*Hurry up, so we can get out of here before the bear eats us!*"

Soon, Darla and Chipper were charging up to the bicycle. Darla leapt onto the seat behind Freddie, followed by Chipper. Freddie handed Mr. Chewy to Darla.

"Go, go, go!" Chipper shrieked. "That bear is still after us!"

Freddie began to pedal, and the bike began to move. He steered along the side of the lake on the hard-packed ground. The craft bounced and jolted.

Darla glanced over her shoulder. "Faster, Freddie, faster!" she screeched. "That thing is still after us!"

The bear wasn't very far away, either.

The front wheel of the bicycle left the ground.

The bear was only a few feet behind.
The rear wheel left the ground.
The bear growled and snarled.

"Higher!" Chipper said. "I can feel the bear breathing behind me! His breath stinks, too!"

Suddenly, the bear lunged . . . just as Freddie gave a powerful push on the bike pedals. The craft lurched to the side, then up and away . . . leaving the bear fuming on the ground as the three children and cat escaped unharmed.

"Oh my gosh!" Darla exclaimed. She was out of breath from running so hard. "That bear almost had us for lunch!"

Freddie continued pumping away at the pedals. Soon, the bike was over the trees, gliding through the air.

"We should be able to spot our houses in a moment," Freddie said. "As soon as we get a little bit higher."

"I'm just glad we don't have a bear chasing us anymore," Chipper said. "That thing was *really* mad."

But something *else* was really mad.

And at that very moment, it was chasing them . . . Freddie, Darla, and Chipper just didn't know it yet.

Two seconds later, they found out what it was.

10

A sudden shadow swept over them like a monster.

There was a loud screech.

And a flapping of wings.

Big wings.

Freddie, Darla, and Chipper looked up . . . and saw the biggest bird they had ever seen in their lives.

"It's an eagle!" Freddie said.

"And he's after us!" Darla exclaimed.

"Maybe he's friends with the bear!" Chipper shouted.

The eagle swooped down again, baring its sharp talons and open beak. It let out another terrible screech.

"There!" Darla said, pointing. "It's a nest! We're too close to the nest, and the eagle is mad at us!"

Darla was right. Not far away, in the crook of a large, old tree, was a huge nest. Two eaglets were sitting in it, staring back at the children with wide eyes.

"We've got to get away from the nest!" Chipper shouted. "Steer us away, Freddie! Steer us away!"

"I'm trying! I'm trying!" Freddie shouted back. He turned the handlebars, and the fantastic flying bicycle suddenly veered to the left. Then he slowed his pedaling and the craft dropped. He turned the handlebars again and began pumping the pedals. Soon, they could no longer see the nest.

Satisfied that the danger was past, the eagle flew off. Soon, it could be seen circling its nest, letting out a shriek every so often to warn others to stay away.

"That was another close one," Freddie

said.

"We've had a lot of close ones," Darla said. "In fact, I don't want to have any more close ones. I want to go home."

"Me, too," Chipper agreed.

"I'll climb a bit higher so we can see over the treetops," Freddie said. "I'm sure we'll be able to see which way to go."

Freddie pedaled harder still. The fantastic flying bicycle rose up, higher, higher still, over the tops of the trees.

And that's when they started to feel raindrops.

Big raindrops.

Only then did they realize that a storm was coming. Behind them, dark clouds had gathered. The wind began to blow harder, tossing the flying bike up and down.

"H . . . hey, Freddie," Chipper stammered. "Do you think we should land?"

"Not yet," Freddie said. "I can't see my house yet. I think we're heading in the right direction."

A strong gust of wind lifted the bike higher into the air. Another gust knocked it sideways, nearly tipping it over. Still another gust of wind pushed it down again, toward the trees below.

"Freddie, maybe we should land," Darla said. "It's getting really windy. What if the chain breaks again?"

"It won't," Freddy said confidently. "I fixed it real good."

"Yeah, but—"

Darla never got a chance to finish her sentence. A terrible gust of wind grasped the flying bike and tossed it about like a toy. Freddie, Darla, Chipper, and Mr. Chewy were thrown sideways, up, down, down more, more . . . .

"Freddie!" Chipper cried. "We're headed for that tree! Do something!"

"The wind is too strong!" Freddie shouted back. "I . . . I can't get control of the bike!"

Up until now, they had been really lucky. They had dodged a plane and crashed into a lake. They had even outran a scary bear and escaped from a mad eagle.

But now they knew that they were going to crash into the tree.

"Hold on tight!" Freddie managed to shout.

And that was all he had time to say. In the next instant, the bike and its four helpless passengers crashed into the top of the pine tree.

11

Branches snapped. Pine needles scraped. Freddie, Darla, Chipper, and Mr. Chewy were tossed into the tree. The fantastic flying bicycle was no longer flying, but hanging on a branch.

And were it not for the thick branches of the pine tree, all of the passengers would have been in a lot more trouble than what they were already in. Because the branches were thick and strong, miraculously, no one fell. Even Mr. Chewy was safe, clinging tightly with his claws. The three first graders were stranded . . . each one holding on to a branch at the top of the pine tree.

A breeze shook the tree, loosening the bicycle. Suddenly, the bike fell. It crashed through the branches before finally hitting the ground below.

"Well, this isn't a lot of fun," Chipper said as he grasped a branch tightly.

"How are we going to get down from here?" Darla asked. "We're way up in the air!"

She was clinging to a large branch near the tree trunk. Mr. Chewy climbed out of her arms and began ambling about, completely unconcerned about being at the top of the tree.

"We climb, that's how we get down," Freddie said. "And we'd better not wait.

It's starting to rain harder."

And it was. The rain was coming down in buckets, making the branches slippery and slick.

"Go slow," Freddie cautioned. "And don't let go of anything."

Slowly, the three friends made their way through the branches. Mr. Chewy had no problem bouncing down, branch to branch, on his own. In fact, he seemed to be having fun.

Finally, they made it safely to the ground. The rain was still coming down hard, so they huddled near the base of the tree where it was much dryer. Nearby, the fantastic flying bicycle lay on its side. The seat was bent, but, other than that, it hadn't been damaged by the crash.

"Now we're in even more trouble than we were before," Darla said. "Not only is it raining, but we're a long ways from home."

"And we don't even know which direction to head," Chipper said.

"And we might get chased by a bear again," Darla said.

"Or maybe an eagle," said Chipper nervously.

"You know," Freddie said as the rain began to let up. "The bike isn't badly damaged. I think I can fix it so it'll fly again."

"Are you crazy?!?!" Chipper said. "We've already crashed it into a tree, Freddie! We're lucky to be alive! I'm not flying on that thing again. No way, no how."

"Me neither," Darla said, crossing her arms.

"Suit yourselves," Freddie said, and he

walked over to the bike and stood it up. The rain had stopped, and it looked like the sun might come out again.

It didn't take long for Freddie to fix the bike. He straightened the seat and tightened a few bolts and screws. Soon, the fantastic flying bicycle was ready for action.

"Are you guys coming?" Freddie asked. He scooped up Mr. Chewy and sat on the bicycle.

"Nope," Chipper said, shaking his head.

"No way," Darla said.

"Fine," Freddie said. "When I get home, I'll send for help. Until then, keep an eye out for wild bears and eagles."

Darla and Chipper exchanged nervous glances.

"You know," Darla said, "on second thought, maybe I *will* go with you, Freddie."

"Yeah," Chipper chimed in. "Me, too."

Freddie smiled. "Hop on," he said, and Darla and Chipper climbed onto the seat. Freddie handed Mr. Chewy to Darla.

"We'll make it home this time," Freddie said as he began to pedal. "Everything will be fine. I promise."

But Freddie was wrong.

Because everything *wasn't* going to be fine. As a matter of fact, things were just about to get worse.

A *lot* worse.

12

Soon, the fantastic flying bicycle was airborne again. Freddie, Darla, Chipper, and Mr. Chewy were again gliding over the treetops.

"Look," Darla said, pointing to some homes in the distance. "There's the city! We're on our way home!"

As they drew closer, more homes and buildings appeared. Finally, Freddie recognized his house.

"Over there!" he said, turning the bike to the left a tiny bit. "I can see my house! Yours, too, Darla!"

Sure enough, they could make out their homes on Fudgewhipple Street.

"I don't think I've ever been so glad to be home," Chipper said.

"Me, too," Darla agreed.

"Land this thing, real quick-like, Freddie," Chipper said.

"Well, we don't want to go too fast," Freddie said. "We'll come in slow and careful, and land on the sidewalk. Maybe even some of the other kids on the block will see us."

"We'll be famous!" Darla said.

"Yeah!" Chipper said. "We'll be heroes! I don't think there are many kids in our city that have built their own flying bicycle!"

Using the handlebars, Freddie turned the fantastic flying bicycle. He pedaled slower. The bike began to lower, gliding effortlessly toward the earth . . . when disaster struck.

13

Just as Freddie began to make the final turn that would put the bike in line with the sidewalk below, the rope connecting the wing and the handlebars broke.

Suddenly, the bike was out of control, spinning in circles, heading for the hard ground below.

Freddie screamed.

Darla screamed louder.

Chipper screamed even louder.

Mr. Chewy meowed and screeched. He covered his eyes with his paws.

"Freddie!" Darla cried. *"Do something!"*

"The steering rope that was connected to the wing broke off!" Freddie replied. *"There's no way to steer!"*

"Tie it back together! Tie it back together!" Chipper wailed.

"Darla! Hold on to the handlebars!"

Darla, still holding Mr. Chewy in her left arm, reached forward with her free hand and grasped the handlebars. It was hard, too, because the bike was falling faster and faster by the second, spinning wildy.

Freddie clung to the bar with his legs, wrapping them around the bar and holding as tightly as he possibly could. This left his hands free to grab the part of the rope that was dangling from the wing. Then, he grabbed the other end that was hanging from the handlebar.

"*Hurry, Freddie, hurry!*" Chipper urged.
"*We're falling fast!*"

Freddie worked as quickly as he could. Finally, when he was sure the rope was tied tight enough, he swung himself back up onto the seat and grabbed the handlebars. Darla released her grip and grabbed Freddie around the waist.

All the while, the fantastic flying bicycle was falling faster and faster and faster.

Freddie started to pedal. He turned the handlebars. The bike responded, steadying a little bit . . . but it was still falling fast.

Freddie pedaled faster.

The bike wasn't dropping so fast.

But the ground was still coming quickly.

Freddie pedaled faster.

Faster still.

But it wasn't good enough. The

fantastic flying bicycle was on course to land on the sidewalk, but they were coming in too fast.

"Hang on tight!" Freddie ordered.

And as soon as he got his words out, the fantastic flying bicycle crashed down onto the sidewalk.

14

Bang!

Kerrunch!

Crash!

Boom!

The fantastic flying bicycle hit the ground so hard that both tires blew. It bounced back up in the air.

Chipper fell off the back.

Darla fell off the side.

Mr. Chewy was sent flying, but he

landed on his feet in the grass.

Freddie was sent sailing over the handlebars, and he, too, landed in the grass.

The fantastic flying bicycle tumbled sideways, twisted, then fell over, finally coming to a stop right in front of Freddie's driveway.

And amazingly, no one was hurt. Darla had grass stains on her pants, and Chipper's shirt was torn a little bit. Freddie's hair was messed up.

"I can't believe we didn't get killed!" Darla exclaimed.

"Yeah, me, too," Chipper said.

"It doesn't look like we'll be doing any more flying," Freddie said glumly as he stared at what was left of the fantastic flying bicycle. Both wings were broken, and the fan had fallen completely off. It was smashed in a dozen pieces on the sidewalk.

The bike itself, however, wasn't in too bad of shape. Freddie thought that if he got new tires, the bike would probably be almost as good as new.

Almost.

"I'm hungry," Darla said.

"I'm starved," Chipper said.

Mr. Chewy meowed.

Darla went home for lunch. So did Chipper. Freddie and Mr. Chewy did the same.

After Freddie gave Mr. Chewy a can of cat food, he went in to the kitchen.

"There you are," his mother said. "I've made you a sandwich. I was just getting ready to call you in for lunch."

"Thanks, Mom," Freddie said. "I'm really hungry." He took a seat at the kitchen table.

"So, what have you been doing all

morning?" Freddie's mother asked.

"Fun stuff," Freddie said. "We put wings on my bike. Then Darla and Chipper and Mr. Chewy and I went flying. We almost hit a plane! Then, we crashed into a lake. Chipper and Darla got chased by a bear. Then we got chased by an eagle. We crashed into a tree, but nobody got hurt."

Freddie took a bite of his sandwich and continued.

"So we climbed out of the tree and fixed the flying bike. We took off again, but the rope connecting the handlebars and the wing broke . . . but I fixed it just in time. We crash-landed on the sidewalk, but not too bad. That's how my hair got messed up."

Freddie's mother shook her head. She smiled. "I just don't know where you get your imagination, Freddie Fernortner," she said, shaking her head.

Freddie shrugged. His mom knew that he was a very smart boy, but she usually didn't believe him when he told her about his adventures. She always thought that he was making things up.

Later that day, Freddie walked to the library. Freddie liked to read. His favorite kind of books were the really scary ones.

"Excuse me," he asked the librarian at the front desk. "But can you show me where the scary book section is?"

The librarian pointed. "You'll find plenty of scary books over there," she said. "But remember . . . don't read them after dark. They are very, very scary."

Cool, thought Freddie. He walked to the scary book section, where he spent nearly an hour looking at the many kinds of scary books on the shelves. Books about ghosts and haunted houses were his favorite, and he found one that looked good.

He checked it out at the front desk, then left the library.

And began walking home.

Thinking about scary stories.

When suddenly, he got an idea.

A *good* idea.

An idea so good that he ran all the way home.

He dropped his scary book on the counter.

Then, he called Darla on the phone. "Darla!" he exclaimed. "I've got a great idea! You've got to come over so I can tell you about it!"

Then, he called Chipper.

"Chipper!" he nearly shouted into the phone. "I've got a really cool idea! Come over right now so I can tell you about it!"

The three gathered in Freddie's front yard. Freddie was carrying his scary book.

He showed it to Darla and Chipper.

"What's your idea?" Darla asked as she handed the book back to Freddie.

"My dad has a tent," he said. "We can set it up in our back yard. Tonight, after it gets really dark, we can sit in the tent and read scary stories with a flashlight!"

"That would be cool!" Chipper exclaimed.

"That would be a ton of fun!" Darla said.

"Let's go set the tent up right now," Freddie said. "Then, all we have to do is wait until it gets dark! We'll have a lot of fun reading my scary book out loud!"

And Freddie was right.

They were all going to have a lot of fun that night.

For a while, at least.

Until something happened.

Something scary.

Something terrifying.

Something that wasn't a story.

Something that was *real*.

And for Freddie Fernortner, fearless first grader, it would be a night that he, Darla, and Chipper wouldn't soon forget . . . .

NEXT:
FREDDIE FERNORTNER,
FEARLESS FIRST GRADER

BOOK TWO:

THE SUPER-SCARY
NIGHT THINGY

CONTINUE ON TO READ
THE FIRST CHAPTER FOR
FREE!

1

"Help me get this tent into the back yard," Freddie Fernortner said to his two friends, Darla and Chipper. The three first graders were in Freddie's garage, where they had just found the Fernortner's small tent. Sometimes, Freddie and his family used it when they went camping.

Tonight, however, the three children were going to use the tent for a different reason.

They were going to set up the tent in Freddie's back yard.

Then, they would wait until it got dark.

Until the shadows grew long.

Until the crickets started chirping, and bats flitted through the sky.

Until the big silvery moon gazed down upon them.

Then, they were going to go into the tent and read scary stories from a book that Freddie had checked out from the local library.

In the dark, with only a flashlight.

"Gosh, this thing is heavy," Chipper said as he helped Freddie with the tent. Darla was carrying the long, wooden stakes. Mr. Chewy, Freddie's cat, was sitting near the garage door, chewing on a wad of gum and blowing bubbles. He was the only cat in the world who could do that, and Freddie was quite proud of himself for teaching the animal how to do it.

And that's how the cat got his name.

Mr. Chewy.

The three kids carried the tent and the stakes into the back yard.

"We need to set it up in a place that will be spooky," Freddie said.

"How can a back yard be spooky?" Darla said, looking around. "There's nothing scary here."

For sure, Freddie's back yard looked a lot like any other back yard. There were several trees, a cement birdbath, and a small inflatable wading pool that Freddie sometimes used during the hot summer days. Near the fence was a picnic table and a barbeque grill, where Freddie's dad often grilled hamburgers and hot dogs on the weekends.

But there wasn't anything that was scary.

"Let's set it up under that tree over there," Chipper said.

"Good idea," Freddie agreed. "It might be even darker under the tree, because the leaves will block out the moon."

It didn't take long to set up the tent. Freddie had helped his father with it many times, and he knew exactly how to put it together. It was dark green and was held up by two wooden stakes and a few small ropes that were fastened to stakes. The stakes were pushed into the ground.

"There," Freddie said as the last stake was pushed into the ground. "Now we're ready."

"Now what?" Darla said.

"Let's meet here just before dark," Freddie said. "I'll get our flashlight that Mom keeps in the kitchen drawer. And I'll bring the scary book that I checked out from the library."

"This is going to be spooky!" Chipper said.

"I can't wait!" said Darla.

"It's going to be fun, that's for sure," Freddie said.

But Freddie, Darla, and Chipper had no idea just how scary the night would turn out to be.

**DON'T MISS
FREDDIE FERNORTNER, FEARLESS FIRST
GRADER**

BOOK 2:

THE SUPER-SCARY NIGHT THINGY!

ABOUT THE AUTHOR

ohnathan Rand has been called 'one of the most prolific authors of the century.' He has authored more than 75 books since the year 2000, with well over 4 million copies in print. His series nclude the incredibly popular **AMERICAN CHILLERS, MICHIGAN CHILLERS, FREDDIE FERNORTNER, FEARLESS FIRST GRADER,** and **THE ADVENTURE CLUB.** He's also co-authored a novel for teens (with Christopher Knight) entitled **PANDEMIA.** When not traveling, Rand lives in northern Michigan with his wife and three dogs. He is also the only author in the world to have a store that sells only his works: **CHILLERMANIA!** is located in Indian River, Michigan and is open year round. Johnathan Rand is not always at the store, but he has been known to drop by frequently. Find out more at:

www.americanchillers.com

Other books by Johnathan Rand:

Michigan Chillers:

#1: Mayhem on Mackinac Island
#2: Terror Stalks Traverse City
#3: Poltergeists of Petoskey
#4: Aliens Attack Alpena
#5: Gargoyles of Gaylord
#6: Strange Spirits of St. Ignace
#7: Kreepy Klowns of Kalamazoo
#8: Dinosaurs Destroy Detroit
#9: Sinister Spiders of Saginaw
#10: Mackinaw City Mummies
#11: Great Lakes Ghost Ship
#12: AuSable Alligators
#13: Gruesome Ghouls of Grand Rapids
#14: Bionic Bats of Bay City
#15: Calumet Copper Creatures
#16: Catastrophe in Caseville

American Chillers:

#1: The Michigan Mega-Monsters
#2: Ogres of Ohio
#3: Florida Fog Phantoms
#4: New York Ninjas
#5: Terrible Tractors of Texas
#6: Invisible Iguanas of Illinois
#7: Wisconsin Werewolves
#8: Minnesota Mall Mannequins
#9: Iron Insects Invade Indiana
#10: Missouri Madhouse
#11: Poisonous Pythons Paralyze Pennsylvania
#12: Dangerous Dolls of Delaware
#13: Virtual Vampires of Vermont
#14: Creepy Condors of California
#15: Nebraska Nightcrawlers
#16: Alien Androids Assault Arizona
#17: South Carolina Sea Creatures
#18: Washington Wax Museum
#19: North Dakota Night Dragons
#20: Mutant Mammoths of Montana
#21: Terrifying Toys of Tennessee
#22: Nuclear Jellyfish of New Jersey
#23: Wicked Velociraptors of West Virginia
#24: Haunting in New Hampshire
#25: Mississippi Megalodon
#26: Oklahoma Outbreak
#27: Kentucky Komodo Dragons
#28: Curse of the Connecticut Coyotes
#29: Oregon Oceanauts

American Chillers (cont'd)

#31: The Nevada Nightmare Novel
#32: Idaho Ice Beast
#33: Monster Mosquitoes of Maine
#34: Savage Dinosaurs of South Dakota
#35: Maniac Martians Marooned in Massachusetts
#36: Carnivorous Crickets of Colorado
#37: The Underground Undead of Utah
#38: The Wicked Waterpark of Wyoming

Freddie Fernortner, Fearless First Grader:

#1: The Fantastic Flying Bicycle
#2: The Super-Scary Night Thingy
#3: A Haunting We Will Go
#4: Freddie's Dog Walking Service
#5: The Big Box Fort
#6: Mr. Chewy's Big Adventure
#7: The Magical Wading Pool
#8: Chipper's Crazy Carnival
#9: Attack of the Dust Bunnies from Outer Space!
#10: The Pond Monster
#11: Tadpole Trouble
#12: Frankenfreddie

Adventure Club series:

#1: Ghost in the Graveyard
#2: Ghost in the Grand
#3: The Haunted Schoolhouse

For Teens:

PANDEMIA: A novel of the bird flu and the end of the world
(written with Christopher Knight)

American Chillers Double Thrillers:

Vampire Nation & Attack of the Monster Venus Melon

Johnathan Rand travels internationally for school visits and book signings! For booking information, call:

1 (231) 238-0338!

www.americanchillers.com

All AudioCraft books are proudly printed, bound, and manufactured in the United States of America, utilizing American resources, labor, and materials.

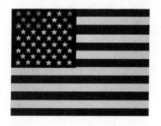

USA

WATCH FOR MORE FREDDIE FERNORTNER, FEARLESS FIRST GRADER BOOKS, COMING SOON!